T0368456

Proctor Jewitz "Master Builder"

Richie Lucas

Illustrations by Shirley J. Clarke

AuthorHouse™
1663 Liberty Drive
Bloomington, IN 47403
www.authorhouse.com
Phone: 833-262-8899

Because of the dynamic nature of the Internet, any web addresses or links contained in this
book may have changed since publication and may no longer be valid. The views expressed
in this work are solely those of the author and do not necessarily reflect the views of
the publisher, and the publisher hereby disclaims any responsibility for them.

Any people depicted in stock imagery provided by Getty Images are models,
and such images are being used for illustrative purposes only.
Certain stock imagery © Getty Images.

This book is printed on acid-free paper.

ISBN: 979-8-8230-3565-1 (sc)
ISBN: 979-8-8230-3566-8 (e)

Library of Congress Control Number: 2024921955

Print information available on the last page.

Published by AuthorHouse 10/16/2024

authorHOUSE®

Proctor Jewitz
"Master Builder"

P.J. what are you building?
I'm building the greatest sandcastle ever seen.
And guess what he truly did.

It made the Guinness book of world records,
And it even had a moat.

P.J. what are you building?
The most awesome soapbox racer ever.
And guess what he did.

It squealed down the track with lightning speed,
He pass through the checker flag with
ease as the crowd screamed.

P.J. what are you building?

A volcano for my science project at school.

And guess what he did.

His teacher and classmates were so amazed,
When the volcano erupted and chocolate
fudge spewed in the air everywhere

P.J. what are you building?
A tree house way high up,
And guess what he did.

Unbelievable from up top you could see,
Clean across the valley amazing!

P.J. what are you building?

A river raft and guess what he did.

He used old oil drums from front and back,

Then rope and plywood he attached.

He used old broom handle sticks,

With dust pans at the end to paddle it.

P.J. what are you building?

I'm building my dog Rex a log cabin dog house.

And guess what he did.

Rex was so happy seems he was actually smiling.
What great friends they are those two.

P.J. what are you building?
A giant kite that looks like a pelican.
And guess what he did.

It flew so high it blocked the sunshine.

Printed in the United States
by Baker & Taylor Publisher Services